CHARLIE FOR PRESIDENT

MICHAEL DENAME

ISBN 978-1-63874-900-4 (paperback)
ISBN 978-1-63874-901-1 (digital)

Christian Faith Publishing, Inc.
832 Park Avenue
Meadville, PA 16335
www.christianfaithpublishing.com

Printed in the United States of America

To my dad, Mike DeName Sr.

One day, Charlie the little Dachshund puppy was watching the presidential elections on the TV. Charlie had an idea in his head: *Wow, I would like to run for president in my community.*

Charlie had his high school diploma, but he knew he needed more than that.

So he decided to continue with his education. He sat down on his computer and began to search for colleges that had classes on government lessons.

So the next day, Charlie enrolled in classes at the local town college.

Charlie began to get very excited on his first day at college. He sat in the classroom listening very carefully to his professor.

His professor was a large German shepherd. He wore a bowtie and thin-rimmed glasses. His name was Professor Harold, who liked Charlie right away.

He could tell that Charlie was smart and eager; actually, all of Charlie's teachers began to enjoy Charlie in their classes.

Charlie learned in his class that in order to run for political office, you needed to start a campaign. First, you needed to start a campaign plan.

He needed to create a message to his voters. He also needed to have someone write his speeches.

He wanted to help his community. Charlie wanted to make improvements in his neighborhood.

He wanted to help the cats and dogs in his district. He did not want them to go hungry and be homeless anymore.

Charlie and his two buddies started working on the campaign. The first step was to advertise and let the community get to know Charlie.

They went to the local "collar store" and purchased supplies to start making flyers. The flyers will be given out throughout the town.

They needed a lot of flyers so they could give them out to the local stores and neighbors.

The three of them went to the park and started putting them on trees and also on all the busy streets so everyone could be sure to read the flyers.

Charlie was happy with the way things were going.

Then one sunny afternoon, Charlie was working on his campaign speech with Pepper.

Pierre, his other friend, came in and told them that Tarzan, the large black-and-white cat, was also running for president.

"Wow," said Pepper. "I know him. He's a really smart cat, and everyone likes him."

So now Charlie knew who he's running against. Charlie told his buddies, "I have to make sure that I write very convincing speeches."

This was important to get a lot of votes.

Election Day was nearing, and there was still a lot of work to be done.

All the flyers were given out, and the speeches were almost all written. Now here was the tough part—raising money.

Charlie and his friends also needed to come up with a catchy slogan. "We should all get along!" was the slogan Charlie came up with.

That was because his community was mostly cats, dogs, birds, and other animals. Charlie wanted everyone to be equal.

Tarzan the cat was running against Charlie and had many voters. So Charlie really had to work hard. Charlie came up with the idea to raise money for his campaign.

So he traveled the neighborhoods in his community. Everyone would gather around to listen to Charlie's speeches.

They were beginning to like him and believe in his promises. So now Charlie and his two buddies that were helping him with his campaign came up with the idea of fundraising.

They decided to get together with a few of their friends and have a picnic at the park. They gave out pins and other treats that said, "Vote Charlie for President."

They drew in a large crowd; dogs, birds, and even cats came from all around to join in the fun. Charlie's pal "Duke," a Great Dane, sold tickets for $1 each.

At the end of the day, they raised a lot of money. Charlie was very pleased with how everything turned out. It had been a very long day but a great one too!

It was almost Election Day, and Charlie was feeling excited but a little nervous too.

Pepper and Pierre were great friends, helping Charlie with all the events and details of the campaign.

Tarzan the cat, who was running against Charlie, was beginning to become very popular among the voters in the community.

Now it was time for getting as many signatures that they could. So Pepper and Pierre went back out onto the streets, giving away pins and flyers, along with the signatures for the ballot.

At the end of the week, they had over one thousand signatures. Charlie was so happy and proud of his friends.

Election Day was only two days away. Tarzan the cat had already picked a vice president.

She was a cute little grey-and-white cat with an attitude. Now, Charlie had to pick a vice president.

They were his two buddies, Pepper and Pierre; he didn't want to hurt their feelings. So he asked his buddy "Leo."

Leo was a Great Dane with a lot of character. Actually, everyone who knew Leo liked him right away.

He was smart and friendly. Leo was very flattered that Charlie chose him. Charlie knew that they would make a great team.

21

Election Day was finally here. Charlie was both nervous and excited.

Charlie and his friends gathered around the television. They were watching the results of the votes all day.

Finally, it was later on in the night. It was a close election. Tarzan was ahead one minute and then the next, Charlie.

The excitement grew in the room as the final votes were in. Charlie stood there waiting to hear the news.

Then all of a sudden, they announced that Charlie was the winner!

Tarzan called Charlie and wished him good luck, and Charlie promised to be the best president ever!

About the Author

Mr. DeName is a Brooklyn-born author who resides with his family pet. A Dachshund named Charlie who was the inspiration for this book.

The title of this book indicates my interest in American politics.

Christian Faith
PUBLISHING

$14.95
ISBN 978-1-63874-900-4